$\mathcal{I}$rie $\mathcal{N}$ursery $\mathcal{R}$hymes for $\mathcal{C}$hildren

This book belongs to

_____

For Teacher Racheal Daley

Drie Nursery Rhymes for Children
By
Black-Sheep M.A.D. ™

Contents

1/Two Weevils Went A Walking

Two weevils went a walking,
One was doing all the talking,
The other was eating cranberry
    sauce.
Both saw the hole ahead,
None turned away, but instead,
Fell head down off the cliff,
One with a buff, the other with a biff.

*Buff/biff — a hard fall

2/ Hoppin', Jumpin' Street Frog

Hoppin', jumpin' street frog,
Hoppin', jumpin' on the log,
No flies to eat, I guess,
No pond to take a rest,
Close your eyes and take a nod,
Stop being so hoppin' mad.

Perhaps tonight you will find a moth,
Perhaps I say,
Or perhaps not.

3/One Step at a Time

One step at a time

The croaking lizard climbed,
The Blue Mahoe Tree in the rain.
Some say it was all in vain,
For as he reached the top,
He fell off plop!
But guess what, he started climbing again.

4/ Mark Anthony had no Money

Mark Anthony had no money,
To buy raisin bread and honey.
So, he sold his hat,
And sold his shoes,
Then cried that he didn't have any.

The baker gave him the raisin bread
    for free.
He stole honey from a bee.
He bought the hat back,
But guess what?

The boy he sold the shoes to had worn it
    to Hope Gardens
To see a matinee.

The ground was hot,
Poor Mark Anthony had to hop,
Crying all the way home.

5/ Fool Hardy

Fool Hardy had a party and invited
  himself alone,

Then stood at his gate and wondered
    if anyone else would come.
He had to eat the entire cake alone, and
    play with the balloons,
While the ice cream melted in the sun.

6/ There Was This Rasta man

There was this Rasta man who had
   a plan,
To see all of creation.
He went to the north pole,
And found it wasn't so cold.

But when he went to the middle of
   the earth,
It was so hot he had to spurt.

He went to the south pole,
And there he caught a cold.
He had fish and bammy with
   some friends,
Before he went back home.

7/Mark and Otis

Mark and Otis left Pedro Cays,
To go fishing on the high seas.
They went so far, they couldn't see land
And caught only enough fish to hold in
    a pan.

They encountered one of the world's
    greatest phenomena.
They rowed fast to make it back to land;
Hot on their trail was the Flying Dutchman,
Who wouldn't mind having as part of their
    crew, two Jamaicans.

8/ The Cat on the Mat

The cat on the mat wore a hat that
   was flat.
In ran a rat, because outside was very hot.
He saw the cat on the mat and cried 'what!'
He screamed and ran back outside!
The cat sighed,
He wondered why,
If only the rat knew he was an irie guy.

9/ All the Roaches

All the roaches in my grandmother's house
   are dead
And all the rats that she once fed.
She never emptied the garbage,
   so they came and filled the house with
   shame.
But now that we have set the bait,
They ate merrily,
Then met their fate.
Now everyone in the family is happy that
   the house is disease free,
Except grandma, who didn't take kindly
   to us killing her company.

10/ While Shepherds Washed their Socks

While shepherds washed their socks by
   night and hung them out to dry,
Some concubines came passing by and said,
   'These socks are mine.'
I must believe, I couldn't believe that a chink
   Is bigger than a flea,
For on the wall, they played football,
   without a referee.

11/ Arthur Northover

Arthur Northover,
Went over yonder,
To look for his grannie,
For he heard she was ill,
After eating mackerel from a tin.

But when he reached his grandma so dear,
There was no reason for despair,
For she was in the kitchen,
Baking chicken patties and bread puddings.

She gave them all to Arthur,
To carry home and share with his brother
and sister,
But he took the long way home,
Ate them all one by one, then threw away
the tray,
Then told his brother and sister, ole gramps
was OK.

12/ Grandma Dor's Kitchen

*T*wo chickens, went into Grandma Dor's
  kitchen,
To see what she was cooking.
They had to canter, and no wonder,
For she wanted to put them into the oven.
She loves stir-fried vegetables and baked
  chicken, and planned to prepare some for
  her grandchildren.

13/ Nosey Parker, Milton Walker

Nosey Parker, Milton Walker,
Peeped through the hole in the wall.
He saw Abigail playing,
But that was just the beginning.
He stuck his finger in,
Something bit him,
And he drew it out crying.

He promised never again to do such a thing.
But did it again when his finger stopped
   hurting.

14/ Benny the Rat

Benny the rat, as a matter of fact,

Lived in the town of Buff Bay.
On the bus he traveled to Kingston,
To buy cheese every day.
One day when he reached Half-Way-Tree,
He found out he didn't carry enough money,
He was angry and hungry, and had to
      settle for a beef patty.

15/ Doctor Bird, Where Are You Going?

Doctor bird where are you going?
Shouldn't you be heading home?
Your children are crying, they're all
   alone.

One fell out the nest,
The other lost her head rest,
And the other two just invited an
   unwanted guest.

16/ Nine Pigs in Wigs

Nine pigs in wigs, walking down Princess
    Street,
Guess who came by, hounding at their feet?
The butcher, with a knife and a bag in his
    hand,
'I have buyers at Coronation Market for
    each and every one.'
Nine pigs in wigs cantered in all directions,
Trying to save their lives, as fast as they
    could.

17/ There Was Once a Man

There was a man, who made his house
from the sand.
He lived on a beach in Negril,
Which was a silly little thing.

The wind blew the sand away,
He rebuilt his house that very same day.

The rain fell and the house leaked,
He promptly patched it with a bed sheet.

The sand was hot from the sun,
He made a fan from coconut bung.

The night was cold, he made a fire and
	warmed himself,
Then played Reggae music on some sea
	shells.

He laughed and said, 'Ha-ha, see, my
	house is here to stay',
Then the waves came and washed it
	all away.

18/Hopscotch, Hopscotch

Hopscotch, hopscotch, one then two,

Hopscotch, hopscotch, I'd like to
      play with you.
You first, me first, it doesn't matter
      who,
Laughing and playing until we're
      blue.
Skipping, and skipping, and skipping along,
Laughing and singing a rhyming song.
Oh, what a wonderful world it is,
When children are truly happy.

19/ Cindy Buckley

Cindy Buckley was very pretty.

She was loved by all the men in the city,
But no one knew who she would marry.
She said no to Muca, because he was not
    tall and dark;
She said no to Eric, who would have
    worked hard to give her milk and honey;
She said no to Andre' - "No Rasta man in
    your life", her mother said.
Then she said no to Dudley, for he didn't
    have enough money.
She went down to North Street, and got a
    man on the beat.

Her mother was so happy,
All her girlfriends thought it was so cool
He attended the right school.
But poor Cindy Buckley was miserable
    and unhappy,
For he treated her like a fool.

TRELAWNEY PIER

20/ Captain Hook

*H*ey look, it's Captain Hook!

He is back for one last adventure
Sailing his ship on the high seas,
And meeting people from different lands
    and cultures.
He went to Africa to see the Pyramid of
    Giza;
He sailed to Europe to greet the Merchants
    of Venice;
Up and down, he walked the Great China
    Wall,

Then off to South America to view the
  ancient civilization of The Norte Chico
  people.
Guess where he just docked?
Trelawney pier in Jamaica!

Made in the USA
Columbia, SC
08 June 2023

17872756R00029